COCO & OLIVE

the COLOR OF LOVE

Michelle Madrid-Branch
with Eviana Tiblet Branch
Illustrated by Erin Darling

It takes a village to raise a book, and we'd like to express gratitude to our *Coco & Olive* team!

Thank you Erin Darling (illustrator), Lindsey McKenzie (graphic designer) and Heather Lei (editor and publicist).
This book would not be possible without each of you sharing your creative eye and sweet passion for this story.

And, thank you to our family and to our pets.
Thank you for your love and laughter.
Your daily reminder of just how beautiful diversity, adoption, and inclusion are gives us hope for a brighter future.

–Michelle & Eviana

Text Copyright © 2019 Michelle Madrid-Branch
Illustration Copyright © 2019 Erin Darling Illustrations

All Rights Reserved.

ISBN 9781796386110

Library of Congress
Cataloging-in-Publication Data available.

Coco & Olive, The Color of Love / by Michelle Madrid-Branch
with Eviana Tiblet Branch; Illustrated by Erin Darling

Summary: A canine mother and daughter pair explore the true color of love and the beauty of family diversity and adoption.

[1. Growing Up & Facts of Life/Family/Adoption - Fiction 2. Animals/Dogs - Fiction]

Printed in USA

For families of every kind and every color.
You are beautiful.

Coco likes to cuddle with her mama, Olive.

Olive likes to weave bright colored blankets at the loom.

When they cuddle and weave together, Coco asks questions.

Lots and lots of questions, like,

"Mama, what is the **COLOR OF LOVE**?"

Well, Coco...

There's a great big door in the place where you were born.

Day after day, I waited at that door for you.

Then, on one rainy morning, the door opened wide and I walked through.

Love is the color of BLUe.

I remember the room where I stood, counting the seconds until I met you.

The walls were painted like pumpkin and spice.

I warmed my paws over a fire's glow.

Our adventure was about to begin!

Love is the color of ORANGE.

Then, I saw you!

All snuggled in a blanket the shade of eucalyptus trees.

Someone kind placed you in my arms.

I pulled you close to me.

You smiled and nodded off to sleep.

So tender, so new.

Love is the color of gReeN.

You giggled at the bubbling water as I filled your bath that day.

Splashing and wiggling while bubbles filled the air!

One landed on your nose, so soft and black.

We laughed with glee.

Love is the color of **EBONY**.

I wrapped you in a fluffy towel and touched your velvety ears.

I could smell the sweet scent of lavender on your fur.

I didn't say a word. I just stared.

Nestled in peace, we sat.

Love is the color of ViOLet.

My journey to you was as magical as the deep, dark sea.

I'm so happy that we became mother and child.

It's written in the shimmering stars, I know.

Love is the color of **iNDigO**.

You slept in my lap, on that plane.

Safe and warm.

Bundled up in a quilt of wild tulips made by your
Grandmother Rose.

So serene and still, I memorized every inch of you.

Love is the color of PiNK.

Family and friends waited at the airport with signs and balloons.

Welcome home!

Joy filled the air. Presents were wrapped in bows.

You were finally here!

Love is the color of yellow.

Now, look at you.

Look at you grow!

It's so fun to watch you run and jump and play.

Reading with you, dancing with you, and tucking you into
bed are treasures stored in my heart.

Love is the color of RED.

"Mama, what is the
COLOR OF FAMILY?"

Coco, family is every color.

Like a rainbow high in the sky.

Family has different tones and textures,
no one family looks alike.

Family has many colors, it can't be
painted of one single hue...

Family is every color.

Family is me and it's you.

We're Coco and Olive.

Mother and child.

A family of browns and vanillas, too...

Spotted and striped, we're all a delight...

Listen close!

Here's a powerful clue.

No matter how much you grow or how far you go,

This is one important truth...

The color of love is us.

My sweet Coco,

Love is me and it's you.

Michelle Madrid-Branch is the author of the critically acclaimed book, *Adoption Means Love: Triumph of the Heart*, and the award-winning children's book, *The Tummy Mummy*. She and her daughter, Eviana, are international adoptees with a passion to share the beauty of family diversity and arms-open-wide inclusivity.

Coco & Olive: The Color of Love is their first children's book together. It's filled with some of their favorite things: bright colors, hints of Africa (where Eviana was born), tender moments between mother and child, and adorable furry friends. Here's a bit of trivia: their dog, Daphne, a.k.a. the best little Fox Terrier on the planet, is the inspiration for Olive. We couldn't think of a kinder mommy for Coco!

Michelle and Eviana live in Santa Barbara, California, with their family and their many pets.

To learn more about Michelle visit www.michellemadridbranch.com.

Connect with Michelle:
Instagram @MichelleMadridBranch
Twitter @LetHerBeGreater

Erin Darling is an illustrator who specializes in developing original animal characters and contemporary storybook scenes. *Coco & Olive: The Color of Love* is her first book. She has been exhibited across the Seattle area and featured in a range of national media publications, both online and in print.

Erin is a self-taught artist who credits her two young daughters for inspiring her to pursue painting, a dream that turned into a career when she unexpectedly became a single mom.

Erin resides in Washington State.

To find out more about Erin visit www.darlingillustrations.com

Connect with Erin:
Instagram, Facebook and Patreon @darlingillustrations.

Made in the USA
Coppell, TX
09 August 2020

32874173R00021